Ricardo Demi

The Adventures of Lucky Rocky

the Magic of Kindness

The Adventures of Lucky Rocky: The Magic of Kindness.

Magic of Discoveries series

Published by Magic of Discoveries LLC.

For permissions contact: magicofdiscoveries@gmail.com

ISBN: 978-1-963328-69-1

Second printing edition 2024.

Disclaimer and Terms of Use:

The author and the publisher do not hold any responsibility for errors, omissions or contrary interpretation of the subject matter herein.

This book is presented solely for motivational and informational purposes.

This book belongs to

_____

_____

Dear Reader!

With utmost respect, I present to you a children's book I wrote, a part of the remarkable "Magic of Discoveries series"!

This book about the adventures of Lucky Rocky the Puppy and his friends easily and effectively teaches the little fidgets about kindness, friendship, mutual help and responsibility and develops their self-confidence and respect for others.

These qualities will help children become happy and successful adults!

Top achievements will boost their self-confidence. Self-confidence will help them cope with all future difficulties more easily. Coping with difficulties is a skill that will definitely be useful to them in the future!

It's true Magic!

Sincerely yours,
Ricardo Demi.

Contents

Part One.
Chicken Trouble

A new day is here. Rocky sat on the porch of his house and watched the ants dragging a large twig to the anthill with curiosity. "That's interesting," the puppy thought, "the ants are so tiny, but they can carry such a large branch. I guess it's because they are very strong and work as a team."

For some reason he wanted to help the hardworking ants. He reached out to them and quietly nudged the branch with his paw. The ants ran in different directions and dropped their load. They clearly didn't understand what was going on. They were running in circles and looking around, as if asking each other: what happened, what happened? Rocky was so big for the ants that they couldn't even notice him. Then the ants calmed down, gathered around the branch again and dragged it into their house. Rocky laughed and decided not to help them again, so as not to bother them.

The puppy sat down cozily on the porch, closed his eyes and turned his muzzle up towards the sun. He loved the morning sun, and the sun loved Rocky. This is probably why he had those beautiful red spots on his fur.

"Hi, Rocky," he heard Brisket's voice nearby. "What are you doing here?"

"Hey, Brisket!" Rocky answered and opened his eyes. "Just basking in the sun!"

"Where's Penny?" asked Brisket.

"I'm here!" Penny said as she walked out of the house. "You're basking in the sun, and I was helping mom," she added proudly.

"Let's play some game," Brisket suggested. "Like hide and seek."

"Hide-and-seek?" Rocky asked. "Let's do it! Alright, who will hide and who will seek?"

"Penny will seek," suggested Brisket, "and you and I will hide!"

"Why am I supposed to seek?" Penny didn't want to agree to it.

"Because you are the smartest one of us!" answered Brisket.

"Ooh," said Penny. "Well then, fine. I'll close my eyes, count to five and start looking for you guys. And you two run and hide!"

Rocky and Brisket nodded in unison.

Penny turned to the wall, closed her eyes and began to count:

"O-o-ne, two-o-o, three-e and..."

Rocky and Brisket quickly ran into the garden and started looking for a place to hide. Rocky decided not to think for too long and simply stood behind the pear tree. Its trunk was pretty wide, and he knew that Penny couldn't see him from where she was standing.

Brisket wanted to hide better to surprise everyone. He saw a large empty water bucket that Grandpa Jose used to water the trees and decided to hide in it. The puppy ran up to the bucket at once, stood up on his hind legs, put his front paws up on the bucket edge and jumped. It is hard to say why instead of jumping into the bucket, he simply clung to it. Maybe he's just didn't push himself off the ground strongly enough or had too much for breakfast? Anyway, he was hanging on to the bucket edge with his front paws and couldn't do anything about it.

With no intention of giving up, Brisket finally decided to get inside the bucket. He grunted and pulled himself up, but then the unexpected happened: the bucket turned over and covered Brisket with a bang.

"A-ah-ah! O-oh-oh! Help me out!" the puppy shouted and started running.

Rocky and Penny heard the strange noise. Penny opened her eyes and Rocky looked out from behind the tree. Both of them saw a bucket running across the yard in front of the house, making strange sounds and kicking up dust. Rocky and Penny were surprised, but Grandpa Jose's chickens peacefully walking around the yard were more surprised than anyone. They saw something strange and huge running straight at them. All the chickens started running, screaming: "Save us! Help us!"

The old cat Roquefort saw the chickens running in different directions, noticed a weird bucket making strange sounds, and then Rocky's and Penny's surprised faces. The cat immediately realized that something terrible was happening! Shouting: "Run for your lives!", he noisily climbed the tree.

There was quite a commotion! Everyone came running to the noise: Grandpa Jose, Rocky's parents, their neighbor Maria, and even the mail carrier Aunt Anita who was passing by. Everyone looked at the bucket, chickens and cat running around the yard, trying to guess what was happening. Grandpa Jose was the first to figure it out, he went up to the bucket and picked it up. Under it, everyone saw poor Brisket, who was completely out of breath.

"Well, well!" said Grandpa. "So, who do we have here?"

"It's me, Brisket, Grandpa Jose!"

"We were just playing hide and seek, and for some reason the bucket fell on me! I couldn't anything since, I was just trying to get out from under it."

Brisket looked around and saw everyone starting at him, Roquefort the cat swinging on the top of a tree, scared chickens looking out from the raspberry bushes, and asked:

"So, what happened? Why are you all gathered here?"

Everyone laughed together as they looked around. Grandpa Jose asked:

"Brisket, are you hurt?"

"No!" Brisket answered, shaking his head.

"Come on," said Grandpa Jose, "I'll treat you to some cookies. And you two should come along, too!" He smiled at Rocky and Penny.

This funny adventure happened in the yard of the old house. Very soon everyone forgot about it, except for the chickens, who now always tried to stay away from the old bucket.

Part Two.
Emma's story

A new day is here. Rocky, Penny and Brisket sat outside Grandma Owl's house, waiting for her to return. She warned the puppies that she would to be out of the house.

"If you come tomorrow and I'm not here, just wait for me," said Grandma Beatrice. "I'll be back soon!"

That's why her friends weren't worried when they did not find her at home. Everyone went about their business. Brisket decided to take a walk around the oak tree. Penny looked closely at the growing flowers nearby, and Rocky sat and watched the butterflies. The butterflies were flying from flower to flower and looked very beautiful. Rocky always loved to observe everything and then think about what he saw.

"I wonder," he said, more to himself than to others, "how these butterflies manage to fly so easily. It must be wonderful to live like that, just flying wherever you want!"

"Flying wherever you want and eating whatever you want!" Brisket, who came up to them, continued his thought. He smelled the delicious cookies from Grandma Owl's house and all he could think about was food.

"Do you think it's easy to become a butterfly?" Penny asked. "You need to work very hard to become a butterfly! Did you know that all butterflies used to be caterpillars?"

"Caterpillars?" Rocky asked in surprise.

"Those green caterpillars that only crawl, eat and can't fly?" Brisket was surprised. "This can't be!"

"It can," Penny said. "My mother read about it to me in a book."

Then the puppies saw the Owl coming back.

"Hi, Rocky, Penny and Brisket!" Grandma Beatrice greeted them.

"Hello, Grandma Owl!" the friends answered her together.

Then they all entered the house, and Brisket was quick to sit down on the chair closest to the cookies.

"Grandma Owl," Rocky began, "is it true that all butterflies were caterpillars at first?"

"It's true," answered the Owl. "I once knew a little caterpillar that later turned into a beautiful butterfly."

"See?! I told you!" Penny said. "And you didn't believe me!"

"Tell us a story," Rocky asked.

14

"I'd be glad to!" said Grandma Owl. "Drink your tea, help yourself to cookies and listen."

Grandmother Beatrice poured fragrant tea into cups and began her story.

"In the oak forest, in a small house lived a little caterpillar named Emma. All around her in the same tree lived other tiny caterpillars like her. They all studied at a special school, where they were taught how to turn into butterflies."

Emma was a good caterpillar, but a very impatient one. She never finished what she started. She just didn't have the patience.

When Emma started drawing, she never finished and ended up with a cat without any paws or a tail. When Emma started washing her legs, she washed one, but not the rest. When Emma began to collect her toys in a box, she collected half of them, and the rest remained on the floor. "I'll finish it later," Emma always said and ran on.

Days went on. One day the time has come for the caterpillars to turn into butterflies. Each of them had to find a beautiful tree branch, sew a cocoon from silk threads and attach it to the branch. When everything was ready, they had to climb into the cocoon.

All of Emma's friends have already started their work. They found suitable branches and began to sew cocoons, so that they could later turn into butterflies. Emma also got ready to search for her magical place, but soon she got bored with the search. The caterpillar wanted to play. She went back to her house, saying to herself: "I'll finish everything tomorrow! I still have time!"

A day has passed, and then another. The other caterpillars had already finished sewing their cocoons, but Emma only chose a branch.

"Don't you want to become a butterfly?" asked a ladybug that was passing by.

"Why wouldn't I? I do! I just don't have the patience. It's so boring to do the same thing for a long time," Emma replied.

"You need patience to succeed! I knew two caterpillars who never became butterflies. They kept crawling and could never fly because they never got their job done," the ladybug told her and flew away.

Emma thought about it, but since she didn't have the patience for that either, she said to herself: "I'll think about it tomorrow!" and went back to her house.

At night, the caterpillar had a strange dream, where it found itself in a very beautiful clearing. Wonderful flowers were growing there, and lovely butterflies were flying around them. They circled around and sang songs. Emma wanted to join them, but she was on the ground and did not have the wings to fly up.

"I'm here! I'm here!" Emma shouted to them. "Take me with you! I want to fly and sing songs, like you!"

But no one answered her. The butterflies continued their flight. Emma shouted again and again. But then she realized that they simply couldn't hear her up there.

Emma woke up.

"No, no, no! I don't want to remain a caterpillar! I want to be a butterfly! I want to fly with the others and admire the beautiful flowers," she decided.

The caterpillar barely waited for the sun to rise, grabbed her tools and quickly went to the branch she chose to sew a cocoon. Emma worked day and night, and then another day and another night. She was very tired, but her silk cocoon was ready. It turned out very pretty. Emma climbed into it and fell soundly asleep.

Suddenly the caterpillar woke up. She didn't know how much time had passed. Emma felt like she had slept for a week. The caterpillar climbed out of the cocoon and looked at the morning sun.

"Look," she heard a voice nearby, "this is probably the most beautiful butterfly in our meadow!" Emma looked around and saw the ladybug that she already knew.

"Who are you talking about?" she asked her. "I'm talking about you!" answered the ladybug. "Look at your beautiful wings!"

Emma ran up to a dew drop hanging on a leaf and saw her own reflection. A beautiful butterfly was looking back at her.

"Is this really me?" She couldn't believe it, and her heart beat loudly with joy. "I have become a real butterfly!" Emma looked into the blue sky, spread her wings and flew.

Grandma Owl fell silent.

"So, to become a beautiful butterfly, you need to do your best, and not put things off until the next day," said Penny.

"That's right, Penny! You're very smart," Grandma Beatrice praised her.

Rocky and Brisket wagged their tails with joy.

Thus ended another one of Grandma Owl's stories. Remembering this story in his bed, Rocky realized that patience sometimes helps to make your most cherished dreams come true.

Part Three.
Paula's letter

A new day is here. Rocky and Penny were sitting on their porch in shock. They looked with all their eyes at the chaos in the yard. Sticks and paper scraps were scattered all around. Grandpa Jose's buckets and gardening tools lay overturned on the ground. The raspberry bushes looked as if someone huge has trampled all over them.

"The wind had scattered everything!" Brisket said as he entered the yard and, seeing the confusion on his friends' faces, added: "There was a strong wind at night. Haven't you heard it?"

"No," replied Rocky, "I was sleeping."

"Me too!" Penny said.

"Sound sleep is a sign of health!" Brisket said with an important air. He had heard this clever expression somewhere, but could not remember where.

"Look! What's this?" Rocky pointed to something round lying in the middle of the yard.

"That's an old crow's nest!" answered Roquefort the cat, who was passing by. "It was blown off that tree by the wind."

"Why do you think so?" Penny asked him.

"I don't think so," said the cat. "I know so!" He stretched, arched his back, raised his tail and walked on arrogantly.

"Come on, let's take a closer look," Rocky suggested.

Everyone agreed and walked over to the crow's nest that was lying on the ground. The puppies stopped next to it and began to examine it curiously. The nest was made from old branches that stuck out in different directions. No one has lived in it for a long time. All kinds of different things lay at the bottom of the nest, among the branches and feathers: old newspaper scraps, a broken wristwatch, a piece of fabric, a glove, buttons and glass pebbles.

"Wow!" said Brisket. "There's a whole treasure here!"

"Crows love to dig up and bring different stuff into their nests," Penny explained.

"Look!" Rocky exclaimed. "I think there's a letter stuck in the branches!" He reached over and pulled something out of the nest.

The friends saw an envelope. The crow probably grabbed it from a mailbox or found it on the road and brought it there. The envelope was old but intact, and there was something written on it.

"This is a real letter!" Rocky said and raised it above his head.

"What if it's very important?" Penny suggested. "What if the person who didn't receive it was very upset?" she added.

"Let's take it to the person to whom it was addressed," Brisket said.

"Let's do it!" Rocky agreed. "But how will we find out the address? We can't read!"

The friends looked at each other and realized that they needed help.

"Grandpa Jose can read, and so can Aunt Anita," Penny said, "but they're not here right now."

"Let's take it to Aunt Veronica. I think she will help us!" Rocky suggested.

Very soon all three ran into Aunt Veronica's store.

"Hello, Aunt Veronica," Rocky greeted.

"Hey, Lucky! Hello, Penny and Brisket!" Aunt Veronica answered. "What happened to you?"

"We're here for a reason," said Rocky, showing her the letter and telling its story.

"Of course, I will help you. Well done!" Aunt Veronica praised the puppies.

She read what was written on the envelope and explained it to the puppies. It was the name and address of the person who was supposed to receive the letter. It was Grandma Alba, whom Rocky knew well. Her house was very close.

"Thank you!" the puppies said Aunt Veronica in unison and quickly ran to Grandma Alba's house.

Soon they were at the gate. Grandma Alba was watering flowers in the yard.

"Grandma Alba! We are here to see you!" Rocky shouted.

Grandma saw Rocky, Penny and Brisket standing behind the gate, put down the watering can, and headed towards the puppies. She opened the gate and invited them into the yard. Friends started vying with each other to tell her what happened to them in the morning: about the wind, about the cat and the crow's nest, and about Aunt Veronica. Rocky then solemnly handed the envelope to Grandma Alba.

She took it and read what the outside of the envelope said.

"Yes, this is my address!" she said. "it's a letter from my old and very good childhood friend Paula. Just imagine, she wrote it a whole year ago!"

Grandma Alba sat down on a chair in the yard and began to read. Her friends sat next to her and kept quiet. A little time passed, and Grandma Alba looked up at the puppies. She was very happy.

"Paula and I grew up together in the same small village. We were friends and played together. Then her dad found a good job in a big city, and their whole family moved there. I came to our city when I got married. Paula and I lost touch with each other, but I often thought of her and missed her. Now, thanks to you, I can write to her and we'll meet again!"

Grandma Alba thanked Rocky, Penny and Brisket for a long time. When the puppies were leaving, she gave them a whole box of candy and invited them to come and visit her whenever they wanted.

Thus ended the story about the letter that made Grandma Alba and Grandma Paula happy. Rocky and his friends were also happy, and on the way home they enjoyed delicious candy.

Part Four.
Brave Richie

A new day is here. Rocky, Penny and Brisket hurried along the familiar path to Grandma Beatrice's house. Soon they were ringing the doorbell, and then sitting at the table at Grandma Owl's.

She prepared delicious muffins for them. They smelled so delicious that it even made Brisket dizzy.

"Grandma Owl, will you tell us an interesting story today?" Penny asked.

"What kind of story would you like to hear?" she put another plate of muffins and mugs of milk on the table.

"Tell us about bravery!" Rocky said. He liked this word even though he didn't know what it meant.

As if sensing that, Grandma Beatrice asked: "Do you know what bravery is?"

"Being brave," Penny answered, "is when you're not afraid of anything! All the different heroes — they are brave!"

Grandma Owl smiled and answered:

"That's right, Penny. Although heroes can also be afraid, they can cope with their fear and win. I'll tell you a story about a brave chick named Richie."

"Wow!" Rocky even stood up in his chair. "His name is almost the same as mine."

Grandma Owl smiled again and continued:

"Richie lived in the hollow of a large tree with his mom and dad, two brothers and a sister. The tree stood on the edge of a cliff, so the house had a wonderful view. You could see far, far away. Richie loved looking at the distant hills and the forest, the blue sky and the rising sun.

The chick dreamed that when he learns to fly, he'll be able to travel and see other beautiful places. He was still small and no matter how hard he tried, he could only jump from branch to branch. His wings were not strong enough to fly yet.

Mom and dad flew away every day in search of food. Richie was always left in charge because he was considered the most responsible. Although he himself didn't think so. The chick was only a few minutes older than his brothers and sister and he did not want to look after them at all.

"Mom, why are you always leaving me in charge?" Richie once asked.

"Because you can handle it! And also, because your name is Richie!" mom smiled. "Richie is short for Richard. And Richard means 'a leader!'"

"I'm not a leader at all," Richie thought, but did not say that aloud.

One day, mom and dad told their chicks: "You are not so little anymore, but you can't fly yet. So, when we fly away in search of food, you should keep very quiet and stay inside the nest. A large pine marten came to our forest out of nowhere. It climbs trees and steals chicks. Be very careful!"

The children promised their parents to be quiet, but when mom and dad flew away, Richie's brothers and sister ran out to play on the tree branches.

"Where are you going?!" Richie asked them. "We promised mom and dad to stay at home!"

"It's so boring at home!" answered his sister. "Come play with us, Richie, it's so much fun here!"

The sun was shining, the sky was blue. "What bad thing could happen on a beautiful day like this?" Richie thought and joined the game.

It was so much fun to play! The chicks joked and made a lot of noise. Their ringing laughter echoed far through the forest.

Suddenly Richie saw some movement at the bottom of the tree. He stopped playing and observed carefully.

"Look! Look! There's someone there!" he shouted to his brothers and sister. The game stopped and everyone looked down.

"I don't see anything," said the sister.

"Look!" Richie insisted. "Right there, near the big stump!"

Everyone started looking more closely.

"I see something!" exclaimed one of the brothers.

"Go home quickly," said Richie, "and sit there quietly. I'll go down and take a closer look."

He began to descend, jumping from branch to branch, and his brothers and sister hurried home.

Soon the chick found itself on the lowest branch. Now he could clearly see the large pine marten hiding near an old stump next to his tree. It was dark brown with a yellow stripe on its chest. Richie also saw its sharp teeth and large black eyes.

"Where are mom and dad? How will I manage without them?"

As soon as he thought about that, the marten made a quick move and leaped to the tree where Richie was sitting. A moment later the it began to climb up.

Richie jumped to a higher branch. As he jumped, he helped himself with his wings. He jumped, stopped, looked at the marten and, when it approached, jumped a little higher. He tried to figure out what to do next.

Gradually the chick calmed down a little. He needed a plan. He couldn't allow the marten to find their nest, which was dangerously close to the tree trunk.

"I need to lead the marten away from my brothers and sister. But how can I do that?"

Well, Richie did come up with a plan. It seemed like a good plan to him, but in order for it to work, the marten must look at him, and only at him. "I need to make it angry," he decided. "Then it will only want to catch me and won't look for others."

"Hey!" he shouted. "How are you doing? Actually, you're not that scary at all."

The marten continued to climb up slowly, and did not reply.

"Come on, climb a little faster," Richie continued to taunt it. "Do you need me to help you up?"

Once again, the marten did not answer, only growled and continued to climb higher and higher.

Richie was also moving higher. He jumped more and more confidently from branch to branch. Actually, he wasn't even jumping, he was flying a little! He began to have a better sense of his wings, and they were really helping him.

"We almost reached our home branch," Richie thought. "I have to make the marten even angrier!" The chick looked around and saw acorns hanging on the tree. They were big and heavy. "That's exactly what I need!" Richie decided. He started picking acorns and throwing them at the marten.

The first acorn flew straight into its forehead, the second hit it on the nose! The marten growled and opened its mouth, about to say something, but a third acorn flew straight into its mouth. The marten choked on it, started coughing and almost fell out of the tree.

"Oh, did you choke?" Richie shouted to the marten. "You've got to be more careful!"

He realized that his plan had worked. The marten was very angry and could no longer think about anything except catching this annoying chick.

So, they rose higher and higher, the branches became thinner and began to bend under the marten's weight. Soon they were at the very top branch. It was thin and leaned towards the edge of the cliff on which the tree stood. Richie was on the very end of the branch, only his wings were helping him keep his balance. The further the marten crawled, the more the branch swayed and bent. Even Richie had a hard time holding onto it.

"Now I will eat you up!" marten growled. "You don't know how to fly, and there's nowhere else to jump!"

Richie wasn't scared. To tease the marten even more, he shouted:

"I'm Richie! My name is Richie and I'm not afraid of you!"

The marten jumped at him, and he pushed himself off the branch, spread his wings and jumped off to the side. Richie saw the marten's surprised eyes when the thin branch could not withstand its weight and broke off. That's how it fell into the abyss — with its big eyes rounded with surprise.

The chick expected to follow it, but he did not fall. He was flying! His strengthened wings kept him above the ground! It was the happiest day of his life! Richie defeated the evil marten and learned to fly. He was circling above his tree, and it was wonderful!

Grandma Owl fell silent and looked at the puppies. They listened to this story so intently that they even stopped eating.

"That's great!" Rocky exclaimed. "Richie is so brave! Remember how he said to that bad marten: 'I'm Richie!' I would also tell her: 'I'm Rocky!'"

"And I would tell her: 'My name is Brisket!'" Brisket added.

"I would just listen to my parents and stay at home," Penny said calmly.

The puppies said goodbye to Grandma Owl, and on the way back home they imagined themselves as the hero Richie and shouted:

"I'm Richie!"

"I'm Rocky!"

"My name is Brisket!"

"My name is Penny!"

Part Five.
Gift for Grandpa Jose

A new day is here. Rocky, Penny and Brisket ran over to Grandma Beatrice's house as fast as they could. They really needed her wise advice.

The next day was Grandpa Jose's birthday. Rocky found out about it by overhearing their mom and dad talking. He told Penny and Brisket, and everyone decided to give Grandpa Jose a gift. The puppies loved Grandpa and wanted him to feel happy, but they couldn't figure out what to give him. They realized that they needed advice and thought of Grandma Beatrice at once.

Grandma Owl sat them down on a cozy sofa and listened carefully. "Well, well," she said and started thinking.

"It's a good thing you decided to make Grandpa happy. I have an idea! Make something for him with your own hands!" said Grandma Beatrice, and then asked: "Do you know how to draw or sculpt?"

"We know how to draw and sculpt from modeling clay," Rocky answered.

"But we are better at drawing," Brisket added, remembering how he sculpted a horse, and for some reason his grandmother said: "What a great dog you made!"

"Then draw a picture for Grandpa Jose and give it to him for his birthday," suggested Grandma Beatrice. "Just wait here a minute," she said and went into the next room.

Sitting on the sofa, friends heard her opening and closing some cabinets and repeating: "Well, well."

"I wonder what she is doing in there," Brisket whispered.

A bit later, the Owl came back to the puppies with a large sheet of paper and a box of multi-colored pencils under her wing. Laying out the paper on the table, she looked at the friends.

"So, let's start."

Rocky, Penny and Brisket jumped off the couch and walked over to the table.

"What are we going to draw?" Penny asked.

"It's up to you," Grandma Beatrice moved the box of pencils closer to them.

"I'll draw a table and a birthday cake on it," said Brisket. "It will be a huge cake! And there will be holiday candles in it!"

38

"And I will draw Grandpa Jose and all of us standing around this cake!" Rocky laughed.

"And I'll draw the grass, sun, blue sky and birds," Penny added.

"And I'll help you write the congratulations on the picture," offered Grandma Beatrice.

Everyone agreed and got to work. It was so much fun!

Penny drew very well. She could probably become an artist when she grew up. Rocky did everything slowly. He wanted Grandpa Jose and his friends to come out well. Brisket tried so hard to draw the most delicious cake in the world that he even stuck out his tongue. Grandma Beatrice wrote: "Happy Birthday to Grandpa Jose!" in large letters at the top of the picture.

Soon enough, the picture was ready. Grandma Owl rolled it into a tube, tied it with a red ribbon and gave it to the puppies.

"Thank you!" Rocky and Penny said to her with gratitude, and Brisket added: "Yes, thank you!"

Everyone looked at each other and laughed.

The puppies ran home and couldn't wait for the next day to come. They even went to bed early so that tomorrow would come faster.

In the morning, Rocky, Penny and Brisket ran into Grandpa's room together. They cheerfully presented him with their painting and shouted "Happy birthday!"

Grandpa Jose took his gift, put on his glasses, carefully untied the red ribbon, rolled out the picture and looked at it for a long, long time.

When he turned to the puppies, his face was shining with joy.

"Everything I love is right here!" he said. "My friends, my favorite yard, the sun, and the blue sky!"

"And cake!" Brisket added.

"And cake," grandfather agreed with him and everyone smiled.

The friends hugged Grandpa, and he hugged them all back. Everyone was so happy!

A new day is here!

What adventures are in store for Lucky Rocky?

Find out in our next book!

The Adventures of Lucky Rocky: The Magic of Friendship.

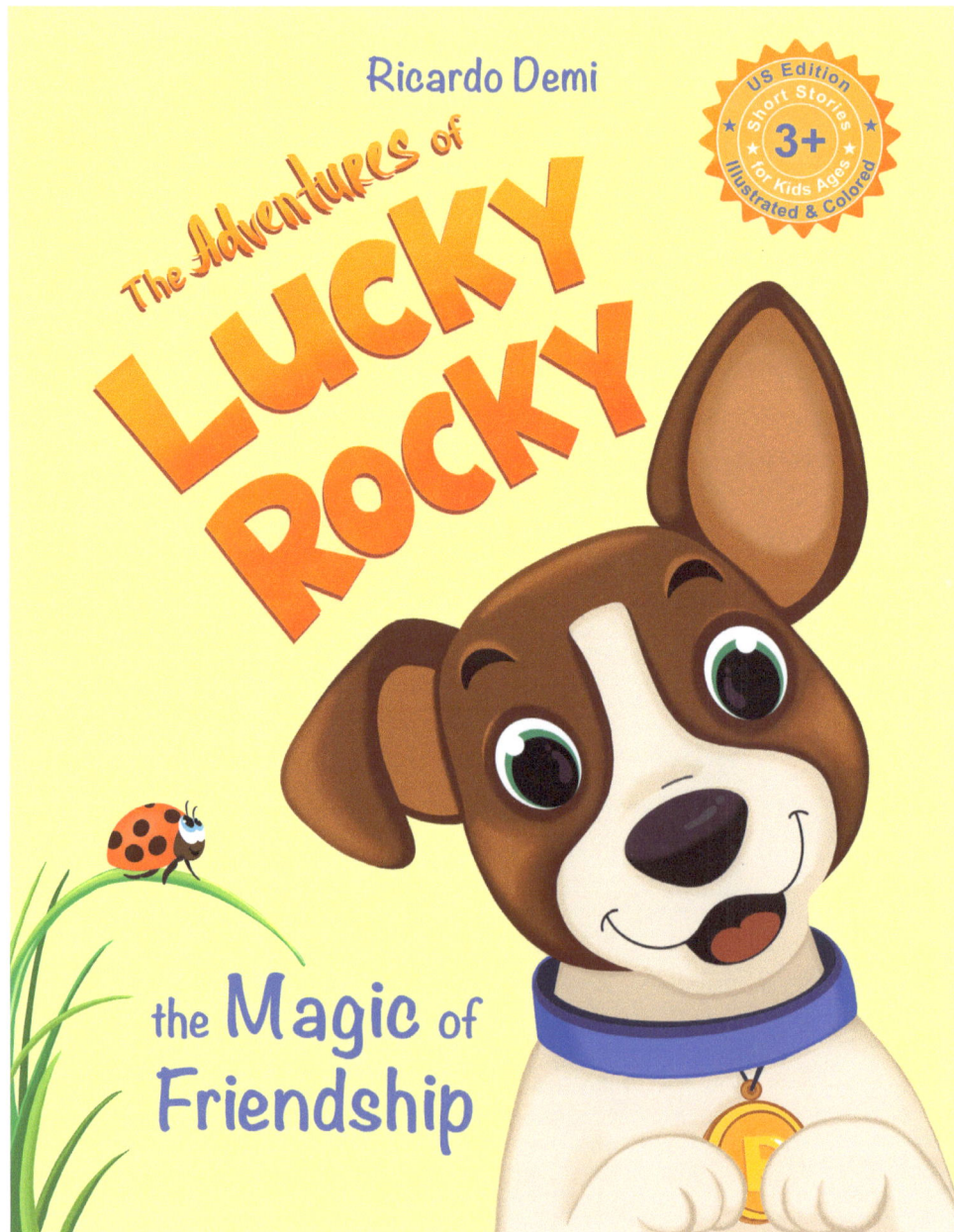

www.ingramcontent.com/pod-product-compliance
Lightning Source LLC
LaVergne TN
LVHW072114070426
835510LV00002B/54